Meet Desert ANIMALS

ARMADILLOS

by Rose Davin

CAPSTONE PRESS
a capstone imprint

Pebble Plus is published by Capstone Press,
1710 Roe Crest Drive, North Mankato, Minnesota 56003
www.mycapstone.com

Library of Congress Cataloging-in-Publication Data
Names: Davin, Rose, author.
Title: Armadillos / by Rose Davin.
Description: North Mankato, Minnesota : Capstone Press, a Capstone imprint, [2017] |
Series: Pebble plus. Meet desert animals | Audience: Ages 4–8. | Audience: K to grade 3.
  | Includes bibliographical references and index.
Identifiers: LCCN 2016035492 | ISBN 9781515746027 (library binding) | ISBN
  9781515746096 (pbk.) | ISBN 9781515746270 (eBook PDF)
Subjects: LCSH: Armadillos—Juvenile literature.
Classification: LCC QL737.E23 D38 2017 | DDC 599.3/12—dc23
LC record available at https://lccn.loc.gov/2016035492

Editorial Credits
Marysa Storm and Alesha Sullivan, editors; Kayla Rossow, designer;
Ruth Smith, media researcher; Kathy McColley, production specialist

Photo Credits
Capstone Press: 6; Deposit Photos: Irisangel, 17; Getty Images: Bianca Lavies/National
Geographic, 15, Bryan Ammons / EyeEm, 13; iStockphoto: Greg Brzezinski, 9, p-pix,
5; naturepl.com: Gabriel Rojo, 19; Shutterstock: Andrea Izzotti, 7, 11, Arto Hakola, 1,
Asian Images, 2, 24, belizar, 21, davemhuntphotography, cover, back cover, optionm, 22,
Svetlana Foote, 24

Note to Parents and Teachers

The Meet Desert Animals set supports national curriculum standards for science
related to life science and ecosystems. This book describes and illustrates armadillos.
The images support early readers in understanding the text. The repetition of words
and phrases helps early readers learn new words. This book also introduces early
readers to subject-specific vocabulary words, which are defined in the Glossary
section. Early readers may need assistance to read some words and to use the Table of
Contents, Glossary, Read More, Internet Sites, Critical Thinking Using the Common
Core, and Index sections of the book.

Printed and bound in China.
007872

TABLE OF CONTENTS

BUSY BUILDERS

An armadillo digs with its sharp claws.

It pushes dirt with its snout.

The armadillo is building a burrow.

It sleeps in its burrow all day.

There are more than 21 kinds
of armadillos. Desert armadillos live
in Argentina and northern Chile.
Some armadillos live in rainforests
or grasslands.

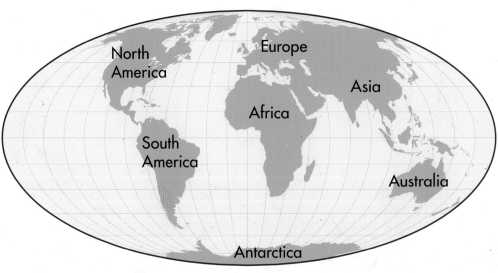

● where desert armadillos live

ANIMALS WITH A SHELL

A hard shell covers grown armadillos' bodies. It is made of small pieces of bone called armor.

Armadillos can be small or big.

Some armadillos are 6 inches (15 centimeters)

long. Others are 5 feet (1.5 meters) long.

TIME TO EAT

At night armadillos hunt for food.

They eat small plants, worms, and insects.

Armadillos get water from their food.

LIFE CYCLE

A baby armadillo is called a pup.

Females have a litter of up to 12 pups.

Newborns have soft, gray shells.

Pups drink their mothers' milk.

Pups stay with their litter
for a few months.
They learn to find food.
After about nine months,
they are fully grown.

Wolves, bears, and coyotes eat armadillos.

But armadillos have ways to keep safe.

They may jump into the air

to surprise predators. Then the armadillos

can run to their burrows.

Some armadillos roll into a ball
to hide from predators. Their armor
keeps their body parts safe.
Armadillos can live up to 30 years.

Glossary

armor—bones, scales, and skin that some animals have on their bodies for protection

burrow—a hole or tunnel in the ground made by an animal

desert—an area that is very dry; deserts do not get much rainfall

grassland—land covered with grass and soft plants

insect—a small animal with a hard outer shell, six legs, three body sections, and two antennae; most insects have wings

litter—a group of small animals born of the same mother at the same time

predator—an animal that eats other animals for food

rainforest—a tropical forest that receives much rain

snout—the long nose of an animal

Read More

Phillips, Dee. *Armadillo's Burrow.* The Hole Truth! Underground Animals. New York: Bearport Publishing, 2013.

Potts, Steve. *Armadillos.* North American Animals. Mankato, Minn.: Capstone Press, 2012.

Schuetz, Kari. *Armadillos.* Backyard Wildlife. Minneapolis: Bellwether Media, 2012.

Internet Sites

FactHound offers a safe, fun way to find Internet sites related to this book. All of the sites on FactHound have been researched by our staff.

Here's all you do:

Visit *www.facthound.com*

Type in this code: 9781515746027

Check out projects, games and lots more at
www.capstonekids.com

Critical Thinking Using the Common Core

1. What is a burrow? (Key Ideas and Details)

2. Why do you think pups stay with their litter? (Integration of Knowledge and Ideas)

3. Explain how its shell can keep an armadillo protected. (Integration of Knowledge and Ideas)

Index